# WARNING

This is a **Total Mayhem** book.

Therefore it is
**not a normal** book.

It is not **just** a chapter
book. It is not **just**
a graphic novel.
It's a bit of both.

When reading it, you will
encounter some things you have
**never** encountered before.

## UNEXPECT THE EXPECTED.

P.S. If you see an
underlined word
anywhere, it means
there's more info on
it in the <u>Almanac</u> at
the back of the book.

# BEFORE YOU READ THIS BOOK
PLEASE READ THIS **VERY**, VERY, *VERY*, **VERY**, VERY VERY *VERY VERY*
# IMPORTANT SAFETY NOTICE:

You may have heard on the news last night that an *unidentified twelve-year-old boy* was recently involved in a **TMSIMSAAMEW** (Total Mayhem Situation Involving Multiple <u>Scallywags</u> And A Marauding Enemy Walrus) *without* having charged the batteries of his **<u>KB-15</u>** in advance.

Because the batteries were not properly charged, his KB-15 did not flash in time. We cannot tell you *exactly* what happened, but we can tell you **this:**

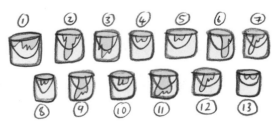

[1] Over *thirteen* buckets of fresh **walrus slime** were involved.

[2] The boy is **fine**, but it was a *supremely* close call. He was rescued at the **VERY** last second by a police **triplocopter** that just happened to be training in the area.

Accordingly, can we *please* remind you to keep your **KB-15 FULLY CHARGED AT** *ALL TIMES.*

If it is not FULLY CHARGED right now, *please* charge it **BEFORE** reading this book.

Thank you.

# THIS IS A TEN-FACED
## *NAG*-OHOFFLE-LOFF-LOFF

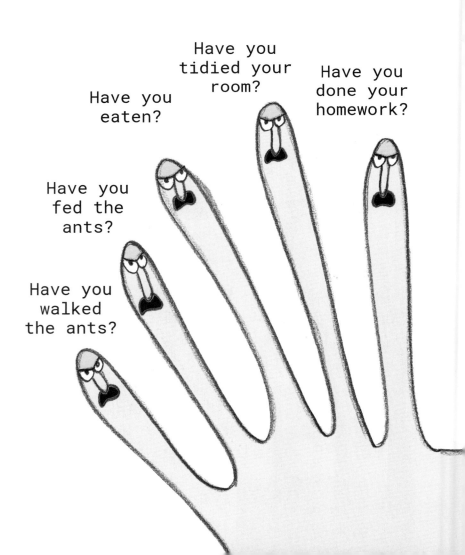

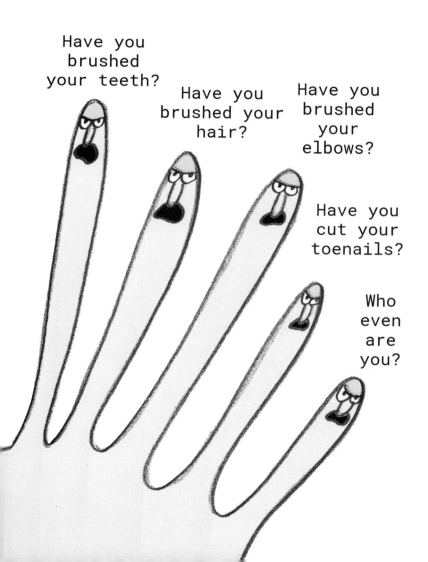

Text and illustrations copyright © 2022
by Lisa Swerling & Ralph Lazar

This book is being published simultaneously in
hardcover by Scholastic Press.

All rights reserved. Published by Scholastic Inc., Publishers
since 1920. SCHOLASTIC and associated logos are trademarks and/
or registered trademarks of Scholastic Inc.
First published by Last Lemon Productions in 2020.

The publisher does not have any control over and does
not assume any responsibility for author or third-party
websites or their content.

ISBN 978-1-338-77047-6

2 2022

Printed in the U.S.A.        23
First printing 2022

Book design by Lisa Swerling & Ralph Lazar

TOTAL MAYHEM BOOK 4
THURSDAY — WAR OF THE
WATERSLIDES

## CONTENTS

*Created by Ralph Lazar*
*Modified, muddled, meddled,*
*mixed, mashed, and modulated*
*by Lisa Swerling*

# CHARACTERS
## Thursday –
## War of the Waterslides

Ms. Glamorgan
*Egyptology teacher*

Dog
*Cat*

Ms. Glissicle
*Waterslide teacher*

Desert-Scallywags
*Enemy fighters*

Rob Newman
*Dash's best friend*

Dash Candoo
*Hero of these stories*

Gronville Honkersmith
*Classmate*

Greta Gretchen-Hoffer
*Classmate*

Vibrating Cockroach of Awfulness (VCA)
*Enemy fighter*

**Shereena Aska-Lonka**
*Classmate*

**Collum Ollum**
*Classmate*

**Mr. Nomsa-Nomsa-Nomsa**
*Hole-Digging teacher*

**Mrs. Rosebank**
*Principal of Swedhump Elementary*

**Mr. Sniffy**
*Special guest*

**Ms. Aqualine**
*Special guest*

**Ms. Grimstead**
*Chief Library Officer*

**Devil-Cat**
*Enemy fighter*

**Jeanjean-Jeanjean-Jeanjean Johnson**
*Classmate, twin of Jonjon*

**Mr. Rrr-Tökk-Tökk**
*Pause teacher*

**Jonjon-Jonjon-Jonjon Johnson**
*Classmate, twin of Jeanjean*

# Chapter 1
# Before Breakfast

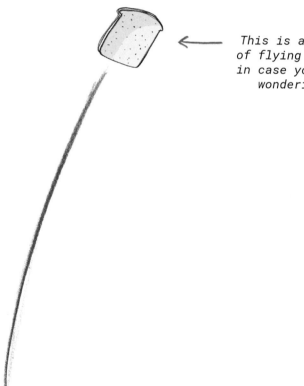

This is a piece
of flying toast,
in case you were
wondering.

It REALLY annoys me when one gets into a **Total Mayhem Situation** before breakfast.

Which is exactly what happened to me this morning.

I was looking forward to
a bowl of <u>snorridge</u>
(which is like porridge,
but made with snow), some
toast, and a glass of
fresh <u>snolly juice</u>.

I had just popped my twelve
slices of bread into the
<u>twoaster</u>,

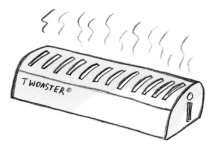

dispensed some snow,

and was sitting down at
the table when...

... my <u>KB-15</u> started
flashing.

In case you didn't
already know, a KB-15 is
a Danger Warning Device.

Danger was close!

I didn't even have time
to prepare.

I went straight to the
kitchen door, opened it,

and there I saw them.

# Seven <u>Desert-Scallywags</u>

and a
## <u>Vibrating Cockroach</u>
## <u>of Awfulness!</u>

They in turn responded
with **Move #26,941**
# (<u>Sandstorm</u>).

This is a
# very, very
dangerous move.

But luckily I'd read about
it in the Almanac.

As the sandstorm grew,
I ran to the **compostables
bin** (which happened to be
filled with some *rather
smelly* food scraps).

COMPOSTABLES
(YARD WASTE
+ FOOD SCRAPS)

Then as the sandstorm
swerved toward me,
I dodged away.

The storm they'd kicked up
hit the bin, which *flipped*
and swirled **up into the air.**

They looked really funny.

I started to laugh.

Desert-Scallywags **HATE**
being laughed at.

They immediately stopped
**Move #26,941 (Sandstorm)**,
and as they did so...

... the bin
came *crashing*
to the
ground...

... and landed **right on top of them!**

All seven were *jam-packed* inside, well and truly trapped.

And by gosh-m'hok it must have smelled bad in there.

Next, I had to deal
with the Vibrating
Cockroach of Awfulness
(VCA for short).

**It immediately attacked.**

I ducked back into the
kitchen and it followed.

As I ran past the
snow maker, I gave it a
good, solid thump.

It started shooting snow
at the VCA.

The crazy creature went
**COMPLETELY KOOKOOBURRAH.**
It had never seen snow
before and had no *idea*
what was going on.

It flew around
*faster* and
*faster*, **totally
freaking out.**

Next thing, the toast was
ready and **all twelve pieces** came
flying out like fireworks on
New Year's Eve.

The VCA got such a
fright that it **flew for
its life.**

As it tried to escape
through the kitchen
door, it **hit** the
compostables bin.

The terrified,
slime-covered scallywags
were released

and went fleeing
after the VCA.

Now it was time to eat
my breakfast.

Soggy pieces of toast
were lying in puddles of
snow, and I didn't want
to be late for school.

Luckily, I had my
**Tie-D-Yupper** on me.

One *click* of the button
and the kitchen was
**sparkling clean!**

And that's how my
day started.

*It was kind of annoying.*

**No toast,** plus my
snorridge had **warmed up to
room temperature.** But
that's what you have to
deal with when you are me.

# Chapter 2

# Assembly

This is a
<u>Staircase Moose</u>,*
in case you were
wondering.

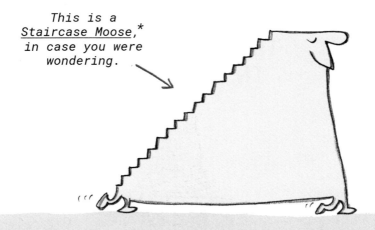

*A moose with a built-in staircase. Obvio!

After breakfast I got changed, packed my bag, and went off to my school, <u>Swedhump Elementary</u>.

**Probably**
**THE BEST SCHOOL**
**IN THE WORLD!**

Greta arrived with a
totally new hairstyle.
**WOW!**
We were amazed. She looked
COMPLETELY different.

"This hairstyle,"
she announced, "is
**The Cleopatra!**"

I was a bit confused, then
I remembered that today we
had **Egyptology** class —
and Greta loves EVERYTHING
to do with ancient Egypt.

Then Rob arrived.

No changes to his hair,
fortunately. At least,
as far as I could tell.

*Because Rob never goes
anywhere without his hat!*

We walked together to the
blacktop, where there
was going to be a *special
announcement*.

Mrs. Rosebank,
our principal, walked up
Harold the Staircase Moose
(*who also doubles as a
stage*) and announced:

**MS. AQUALINE!** She was the owner of the new <u>Aqualinia Water Park</u> that had just opened next to the <u>Sniffsonian Museum</u>.

If you haven't been there, you should — it's

# FANTASTIC!

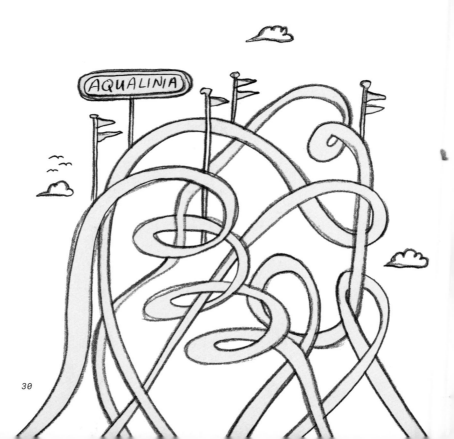

Ms. Aqualine made her way up Harold.

**Everyone cheered.**

But just as she was about to speak, we heard a *buzzing* in the sky.

Was it a swarm of
<u>invizizzes</u>?

No!

Suddenly, a **helicopter**
appeared above us.

It was coming in to land,
and *quickly*.

What a strange-looking
thing!

And then I realized.
It wasn't a normal
helicopter.

It was a **boreholicopter** –
a helicopter that can also
dig tunnels!

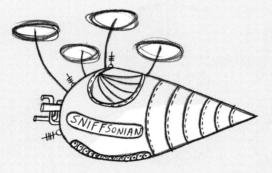

# Amazing!

I'd heard of them
but had never seen one.

They are **very expensive**
and *very rare*.

As it came closer, we saw, emblazoned clearly on its side, the word *SNIFFSONIAN*!

The wheels came down,
propellers retracted,
the hatch slid open, and
out of it popped...

... **Mr. Sniffy himself**,
owner of the *Sniffsonian*,
the world's most **famous** and
**important** museum of natural
history, artifacts, trivia,
miscellany, and heemo-globule
globules.

It is also famous for its
*epic cafeteria*.

# "Hello, everyone!"
## he shouted.

"I'm Mr. Sniffy,
your *SECOND special guest*
for the day!"

If we could have seen
Mrs. Rosebank's face, I'm
not sure what it would
have expressed.

**Surprise or delight?**

Or *both*?

**Two** special visitors in
one day!

Once the dust had settled,
Ms. Aqualine resumed her
introduction.

She explained that there was space for *ONE more slide* in her water park.

She was having a *competition* for the kids at our school, to see who could come up with the **BEST IDEA** for a
# *NEW WATERSLIDE!*

We should put our entries into her **Amazing Ideas Box** at the start of Waterslide class, and she'd announce the winner *at the end of the day.*

The winner's idea would be
turned into an
*ACTUAL waterslide!*

We all looked at each
other and smiled.

Mr. Sniffy,
Special Guest #2,
smiled too.

This was **VERY exciting.**

*Can you imagine?*
You come up with a good
idea and next thing
**that idea is reality!**

# Chapter 3

# Pause Class

Dog

We went off happily to
first period —
# Pause Class.

And don't ask me why the
Pause building is shaped
like a giant noodle,
because *I have no idea.*

Let me introduce our
Pause teacher,
**Mr. Rrr-Tökk-Tökk.**

Not only did he win the
**Pause Game World
Championships**,
he actually *invented*
the Pause Game,
and of course wrote the
*#1 bestseller* Pauselopedia.

As we walked into class,
we couldn't help but notice a
VERY *delicious*-looking
**armadillo cake!**

Mr. Rrr-Tökk-Tökk
explained excitedly:
"**It's my birthday today!!**
So at the end of the lesson
we're all eating cake!
**Happy birthday to ME!!**"

Once we'd settled down,
the lesson began.
Mr. Rrr-Tökk-Tökk went over
the rules of the Pause Game,
even though we've all played
it since we were old enough
to speak.

*(In fact, "Pause!" was
Collum Ollum's first word.)*

**RULE 1:** When someone
shouts "Pause!" everyone
in the room has to

completely still
including the person who
shouted "Pause!"

**RULE 2:** You can only move again when the shouter shouts:

**RULE 3:** The shouter needs *to hold their breath between* shouting "Pause!" and "Play!"

**RULE 4:** If the shouter *breathes* before they say "Play!" the "Pause!" is broken and everyone can move again.

**RULE 5:** Each person is only allowed to shout "Pause!" *once per day*, and they can do it whenever they want.

The game is very *SERIOUS* but also *really fun* and funny, and you should try it yourself if you haven't already.

Today we were learning **Advanced Pause Strategy**.

Mr. Rrr-Tökk-Tökk explained
some Gold-Star Tips for
becoming a Pause Master:

Be **PATIENT.**

Wait for a
**GOOD MOMENT.**

Use the element
of **SURPRISE.**

Totally **FREEZE**
until the shouter
shouts "PLAY!"

And, remember,
always...

... keep **HYDRATED!**"

said Mr. Rrr-Tökk-Tökk as
he went to pour himself a
glass of water.

Collum Ollum, who was not
being especially
**PATIENT**

but had found a
**GOOD MOMENT**

and was using the
**ELEMENT OF SURPRISE,**

shouted:

**PAUSE!**

Of course the water
was *already pouring* and
Mr. Rrr-Tökk-Tökk's arm
was **frozen in place.**

And, as you know, water
has no ears, and so
the water itself **kept
pouring.**

All over the desk.

Mr. Rrr-Tökk-Tökk did not
look too happy.
In fact, he looked furious.

## "WHO DID THAT?"

he shouted, really loudly.

But of course Collum had
not yet shouted **"PLAY!"**
so Mr. Rrr-Tökk-Tökk had
**broken RULE NUMBER 2**
*AND* one of his own
**GOLD-STAR TIPS,**
and things started to
*unravel quite quickly*
from there.

Mrs. Belch-Hick's cat, Dog, had been asleep on the ceiling.

The SHOUT gave Dog **such a fright** that she fell off the ceiling and landed *right on top of* Mr. Rrr-Tökk-Tökk's head.

He **screamed**, which gave
Dog an *even bigger fright*,
so she clung on for dear
life, sinking her claws
deep into his head.

Mr. Rrr-Tökk-Tökk then
**TOTALLY PANICKED,** as he
had no idea what kind of
brain-sucking, hairy
jellyfish was on his head.
He started to run like a
**FLUSTERED WOMBAT**

but **slipped** in the puddle
and went **flying** across
the room, heading *straight
for* the armadillo cake.

# KABOOM!
He hit the shelf.
*The cake went flying*

and landed straight on
*top of Dog*, who was
somehow still attached
to Mr. Rrr-Tökk-Tökk.

The cake then **exploded**
as Dog **FREAKED OUT** and
started flailing like
a *chocolate-covered
Vibrating Cockroach of
Awfulness.*

I told you the
Pause Game was SERIOUS.

(AND *FUN!*)

The lesson was obviously _canceled_, and while we weren't getting any armadillo cake anytime soon, at least we had the last bit of class to start brainstorming waterslide ideas.

The competition was **ON!**

# Chapter 4

# Hole-Digging Class

We have absolutely no idea who this is, in case you were wondering.

Next up was
**Hole-Digging** class.

Our hole-digging teacher
is **Mr. Nomsa-Nomsa-Nomsa.**

*I don't know if it's just
me but does his head seem
to be shaped a little like a
hole-digger, or some kind of
rocket ship about to take off?*

He's the world's most
respected <u>hole-digger</u>
mechanic.

He can repair a hole-digger
faster than anyone.
And I mean **anyone**.
If there was a *World
Hole-Digger Repair
Championships,*
he'd win it for sure.

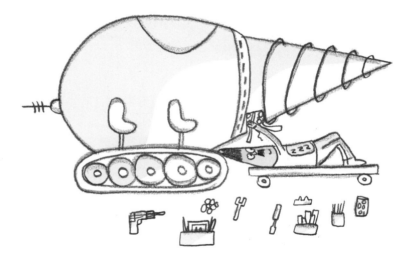

He can repair an
<u>Aardvark 4.2D</u>
(the kind of hole-digger
Rob and I have)
in under five minutes.

William Williams, the Chief Mechanic at our rival school, **Stumpnose Elementary**, once challenged Mr. Nomsa-Nomsa-Nomsa to a **REPAIR DUEL**. It was a race to see who could repair three hole-diggers first:

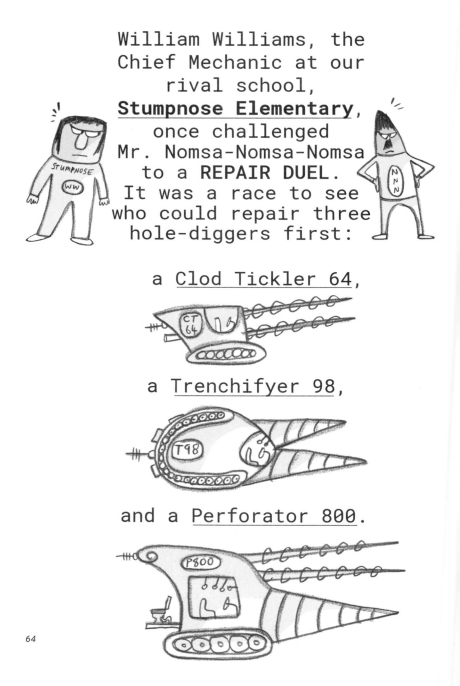

a <u>Clod Tickler 64</u>,

a <u>Trenchifyer 98</u>,

and a <u>Perforator 800</u>.

William Williams got an **early lead** because he had years of experience with *ossified sprocket valves* on the Clod Tickler 64, especially in the *turbo cylinders*, and he was quick with the *slime transfusion*.

But he **fumbled** at the *smolensky valve reconfiguration*, and Mr. Nomsa-Nomsa-Nomsa overtook him.

On the Trenchifyer 98, Williams regained lost time **decoagulating** the *sheep-shank gaskets* and almost caught up.

Finally on to the
Perforator 800:
Nomsa-Nomsa-Nomsa **surged**
ahead during the *kandinsky
filter reinstall*,

and **expanded** his lead
after a *wemnoff inverter
hump* **exploded** in Williams's
hands (don't you just hate
it when that happens?) and
olive oil leaked everywhere.

From that point onward,
Nomsa-Nomsa-Nomsa's lead
**just grew.**

Mr. Nomsa-Nomsa-Nomsa won
by eight minutes and
**was interviewed on TV.**

*Professor-Inspector
Josiah Stumpnose,*
the evil principal of
Stumpnose Elementary
(and William Williams's
boss), was **not happy.**

Apparently he sulked
for *three days and
four minutes.*

Anyway, today's lesson
was **name-digging**, where
we had to dig our names
under the ground.
Mr. Nomsa-Nomsa-Nomsa
split us up in tutus.
I mean, into twos.

Gronville
with Rob.

Collum with
Jonjon-Jonjon-
Jonjon

Shereena with
Jeanjean-Jeanjean-
Jeanjean

I was super-stoked to be
paired with Greta.

Greta + driving + machines =
*Fantastico!*

We were using
# Aardvark 66s,
which are *comfortable*, **silent**,
and *very fast* machines.

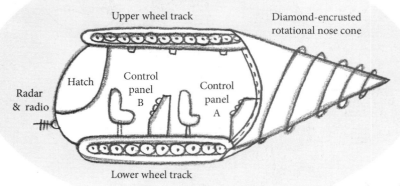

## AARDVARK 66

Upper wheel track

Diamond-encrusted
rotational nose cone

Hatch

Control
panel
B

Control
panel
A

Radar
& radio

Lower wheel track

Down we went, guided
by the Aardvark
<u>3D Macro-map</u>, which is
a map for when you're
exploring underground.

We carved a pretty
perfect GRETA tunnel,
and *started on my name.*

*d...*

*d a*

...*a*...

but as we were about
to start on the *s*,
we suddenly hit
another tunnel!

# What?!

The macro-map didn't
show this tunnel!

It was freshly dug.

Greta swung a sharp UP
into the new tunnel.

Up ahead we saw
another digger!

We snuck up behind until
we were close enough to see
the license plate:

# SNIFF-01

?!WHAT?!

Mr. Sniffy in his
boreholicopter!

# Where was he going?

I rebooted the macro-map
and set it to Mode42F.

It showed that Sniffy was
tunneling **straight** to the
*Sniffsonian Museum.*

What the heggleswick
was he up to?

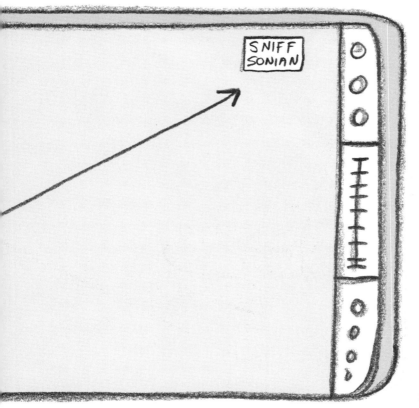

Time was running out,
so we headed back up
to the surface.

Nothing would keep
Greta away from our next
class . . .

# Chapter 5

# Egyptology Class

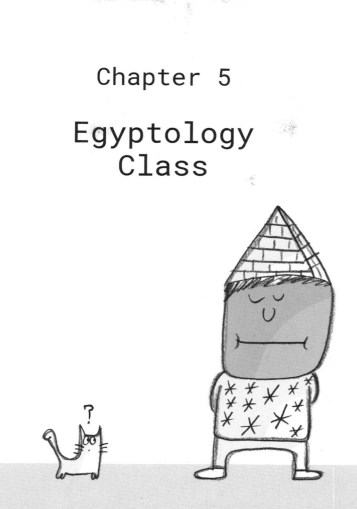

# Our Egyptology teacher is
# Ms. Glamorgan.

She's really, really nice. On some days, especially if it has been raining, there appears to be a **small pyramid** growing out of the top of her head. Nobody is sure whether it is decorative or some kind of pointy pimple.

And of course we'd never ask.

Not only is she a world
expert on Egyptology,
she's also a
**REALLY famous swimmer.**

She has won gold medals
twice at the Olympics.

One for the 99-meter **elbowstroke,**

and one for the 147-meter
**grinning-dolphin.**

She's also the only person to have swum the full length of the River Nile (4,132 miles) five times...using a *DIFFERENT* stroke each time.

## 2020: **Windmill-stroke**

## 2019: **Snack-stroke**

## 2018: **Sulking-duck-stroke**

## 2017: **Confused-starfish-stroke**

## 2016: **Cactus-balancing-stroke**

Ms. Glamorgan really liked
Greta's hairstyle.

Greta beamed.

The lesson was
Hieroglyphics, and
Mr. Sniffy, the
**Guest-Expert-of-Honor,**
was going to show us all
how to write them out.

But Mr. Sniffy had not
shown up.

Greta and I looked at
each other.

*Should we say something?*

Suddenly he burst in,
looking a little
flustered, a little dusty,
a little flusty, and more
than just a little sweaty.

He started the lesson.
And actually he was quite
good at it.

Soon we were all
practicing writing
in hieroglyphics.

Then he instructed us to write
out the phrase that came closest
to the name of the world's most
famous water fountain designer...

**Andri Grimminik** Herr-Groggen-
Chommen-Hummen-Grekken

... in hieroglyphics
of course.

We were all up for the
challenge.

"Right!" I heard Mr. Sniffy
snicker to himself,
"That should keep them
busy for a while!"

*How weird.*

While we were all trying
to work it out, Mr. Sniffy
began pacing around the
room, scribbling on a piece
of parchment.

Then he pulled out his
phone, took a photo of what
he'd written, and — PING! —
sent the photo off.

*How weirder.*

Something felt
**NOT AT ALL RIGHT.**

Didn't he know the rules?
NO PHONES IN CLASS?!

I didn't have much time —
I had to act first.
I quietly took my
**butterfly-cam-drone**
out of my backpack,
activated it, and sent it
over him.

It secretly took a photo
of Sniffy's parchment
and then flew back into
my backpack.

I keep a small printer in my backpack specifically for these occasions, so I printed out the photo.

Sniffy's note was written
*entirely* in some kind of
**crazy homemade hieroglyphics!**

But that wasn't even the
*wildest* part.

On Sniffy's parchment
I could clearly see the
image of a cat.

**And not just any old cat.**

# It had two tails!
## <u>DEVIL-CAT</u>?!

What the
onga-longa-snodwick
was going on?

I passed the photo secretly
to Rob to see if he could
figure out what it meant.

*No idea.*

Then to Greta.

*Nope.*

None of us could
understand it.

The tock was clicking and
the lesson was drawing to
an end.

Mr. Sniffy stood up and
cleared his throat.

Whatever next?

"As a **special treat**,"
he declared,
"for your next class
I'm taking you to...

# ... the Sniffsonian!

I want our **amazing** exhibits to inspire you to come up with **fantastic** waterslide ideas!"

# What a day this was turning out to be!

# Chapter 6

# The Sniffsonian

*This is a sign to the cafeteria, in case you were wondering.*

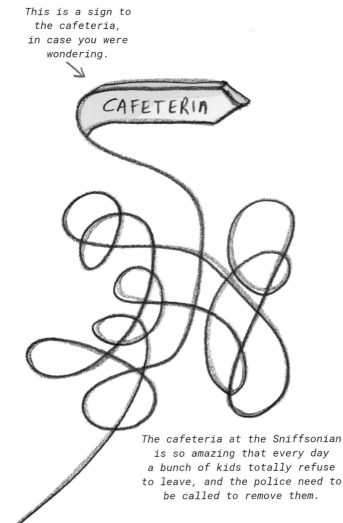

CAFETERIA

*The cafeteria at the Sniffsonian is so amazing that every day a bunch of kids totally refuse to leave, and the police need to be called to remove them.*

We all assembled again on
the blacktop.

The next thing the school
<u>flus</u> arrived, piloted
by none other than
Mr. Hogsbottom!

A flus is like a bus,
but better.

# It can fly!

On the journey, Rob, Greta,
and I tried to work out
Sniffy's message.

Aside from decoding the
cat symbol (which didn't
take a genius), we weren't
having much luck, and the next
thing we knew, we had arrived
at the museum.

Decoding the rest of the
message would have to wait.

"Follow me!"
yelled Mr. Sniffy as he
rushed us through the EPIC
# Dinosaur Room,

then the **Volcano Room,**

then the **Rainforest Room,**

and then the **Slime Room,**

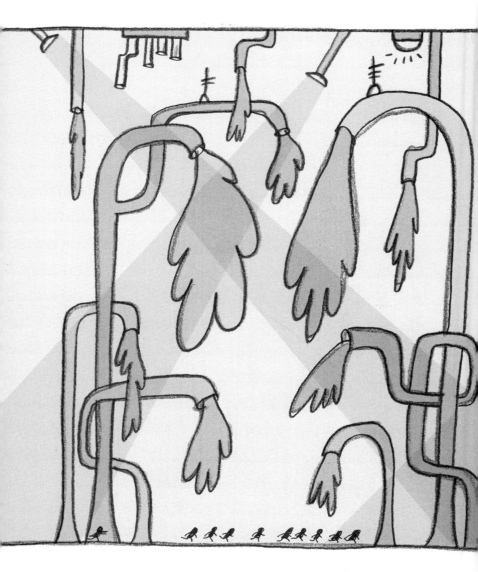

and then the **Cloud Room.**

Finally, out of breath,
we arrived in the
**Ancient Egypt Room.**

"The tour is OVER, kids!"
Mr. Sniffy declared.

We looked at each other,
confused. *So soon?*

"I wanted to leave you plenty of time to finish off your waterslide competition ideas!" he told us.

"You can work in the cafeteria, and of course feel free to help yourselves to the many, many snacks.

I hope the **amazingness of the Sniffsonian Museum** has inspired you!"

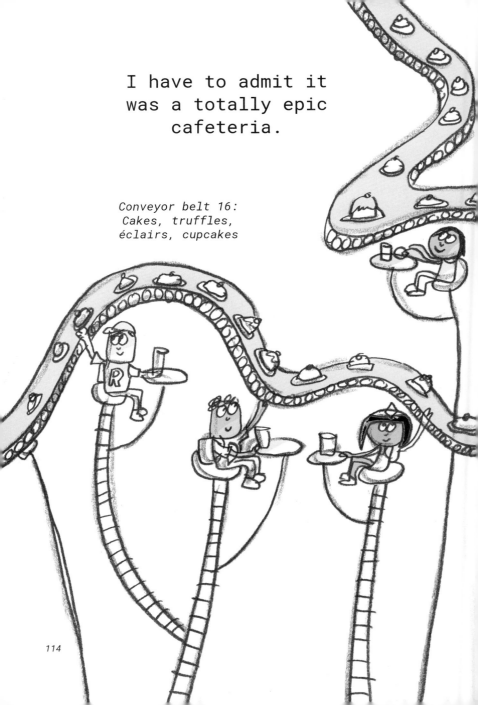

I have to admit it
was a totally epic
cafeteria.

*Conveyor belt 16:*
*Cakes, truffles,*
*éclairs, cupcakes*

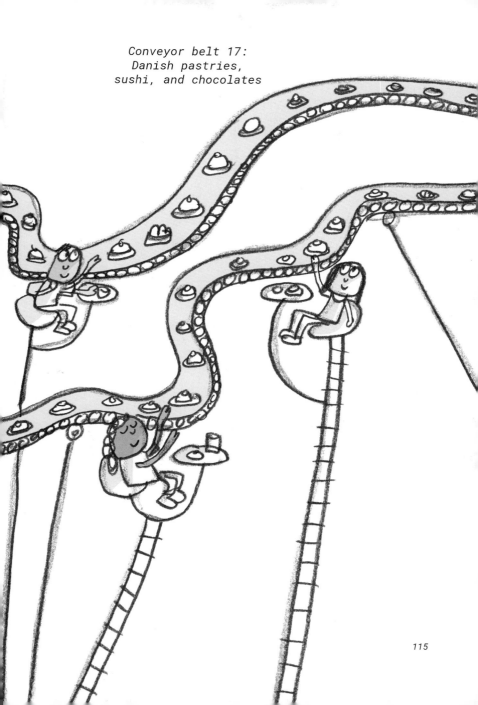

Conveyor belt 17:
Danish pastries,
sushi, and chocolates

115

Greta and I wanted to work on decoding the secret message, but finalizing our *waterslide ideas* was **MUCH more urgent.**

Eventually it was time
to leave.

Mr. Sniffy waved us off.

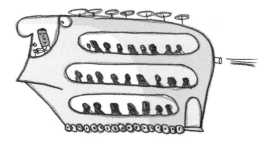

Back to school we flew,
using the last crucial
minutes to finish off
our competition entries.

The *final deadline* to submit
them was the start of
Waterslide Class, up next.

# Chapter 7

# Waterslide Class

*Would you jump?
I totally would.*

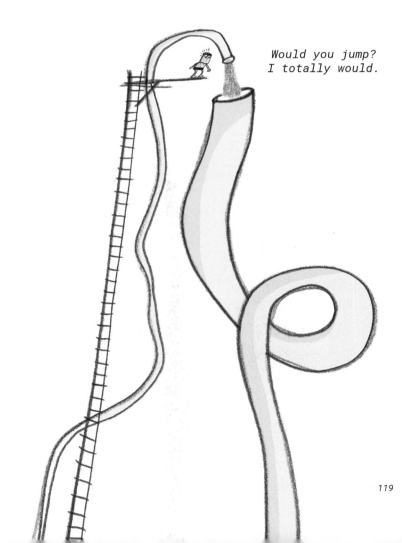

At the entrance to Waterslide
Class stood **Ms. Glissicle**,
our *Waterslide* teacher,
and Ms. Aqualine, with the
Amazing Ideas Box.

Wait, what?! The ideas box
was **exactly the same box** as
the drawing on Mr. Sniffy's
secret message!

**Yes! One more part of the message decoded!**

As we passed her, we *excitedly* slipped our ideas into the slot.

And then off to the
library she headed
to read them all.

Just *one more class* until
**the winner was announced!**

All right! Back to
**Waterslide Class.**

Ms. Glissicle was the
**World Waterslide Champion**
in 2008, the final of
which was held on the
*famously infamous* slide,
**Spaghetti Junction.**

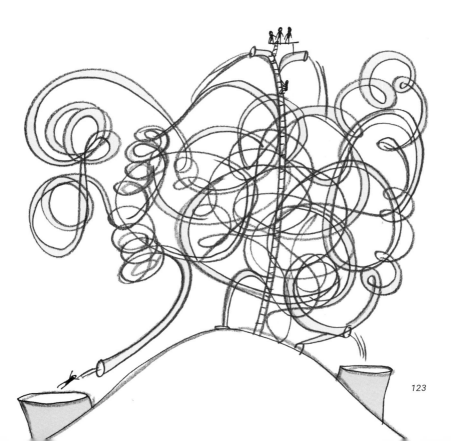

She won by doing a
**Quadruple Corkscrew** off the
shoulder of Tube 617
(known as the **Death
Descent**),

617

whilst balancing
a *cup of tea* on her **head**.

She spilled
*not a single drop.*

Apparently she drank the tea during the awards ceremony, and it was *still warm.*

In today's lesson
we were watching a
documentary about the
***Oshkosh-Woznohokk***
***Waterslide Incident***
***of 1972.***

Obviously you've heard of it.

But just to *refresh* your
*memory*, the Oshkosh-
Woznohokk Waterslide was
built by Oliver Oshkosh and
Wendy Woznohokk.

Soon after its opening, the two best friends had a falling out *(for reasons unknown)* and became **worst enemies** and Wendy Woznohokk went off and built her own slide, right next door to the original.

ORIGINAL
OSHKOSH-WOZNOHOKK
SLIDE

WENDY'S
NEW
WATERSLIDE

Oliver Oshkosh accused
her of stealing his idea,
and a fight ensued during
which both slides
**caught fire** and **BURNED** to
the ground.

Oliver and Wendy were sent to **jail**, but later *escaped* by building a **secret waterslide** from within their cell that led straight to a *waiting boat*.

WORMWOOD SHRUBS
MAXIMUM SECURITY
PRISON

Neither has been heard
from since, but it's
rumored they *got married*,
changed their names, and
**live on an island**
somewhere unknown.

If you do happen to spot
an island somewhere
totally covered in
waterslides, please report
it to your nearest police
station or III (Island
Inspection Inspector).

While the film was running,
Rob, Greta, and I returned to
Mr. Sniffy's secret message.

We were making progress.

We had the **Devil-Cat** and the
**Amazing Ideas Box**.

The third drawing looked
like a building.
And were those books?

A house of books!

Perhaps a library?

# LIBRARY!

And it was our very
next class!

# Chapter 8

# Library Class

This is Ms. Grimstead
heading to the Annual
Regional Librarian Picnic
on her P'tonk-45, in case
you were wondering.

Off to the library to
see who'd won!

Alongside Ms. Grimstead,
the **Chief Library Officer**
of Swedhump Elementary,
stood Ms. Aqualine and
Mrs. Rosebank, and behind
them, several other teachers.

Grodzinski

Zhonst

Woodhouse

Belch-Hick

Tadros

Darling

Hogmanny
Hog-Mahomm

Hogsbottom

Grimstead

Rosebank

Aqualine

In front of them,
on a plinth,
was the

# AMAZING
# IDEAS BOX.

Ms. Aqualine
stood up to
announce the
winner...

... **just** as Rob, Greta, and I made a breakthrough on the last clue!

It looked like a cube of **ICE!**

We were **SO CLOSE...**

... when suddenly, from behind us came a loud, clear shout.

PAUSE!

Of course, WE FROZE!

From *behind*
*the library shelves*

# DEVIL-CAT

and the Desert-Scallywags
appeared. Devil-Cat GRABBED
the Amazing Ideas Box
off the plinth.

The thieves had moved like *a flash of lightning.*

By the time we realized what had happened they'd **already disappeared** into the maze of library shelves.

Mr. Sniffy had sent the coded message **to Devil-Cat!**

The **ICE** drawing was telling Devil-Cat to **FREEZE us all** in the library so he could steal the box of waterslide ideas!

We had solved the last clue, **but TOO LATE!**

From somewhere within
the library we heard
Devil-Cat call:

But of course by then they,
and the box, had *totally*
and *completely* **disappeared.**

Everyone was **REALLY upset**. Especially Ms. Grimstead. Her head lump, which you may remember from *yesterday*, began to **THROB**.

There was general panic in the room. Some of the teachers started *screaming*. Some of the kids began to *cry*. **Library class was canceled for sure.**

Second day in a row!

Rob and I immediately moved into <u>FiCTaP mode</u> (Find Clues, Track, and Pursue).

We scanned the carpet, and there — **sand!**

*A thin trail of it.*

The Desert-Scallywags had *carelessly* left a trail for us to follow!

And so follow it we did.

Through section A, then B, then C.

## At D, I strapped on my KB-15.

Then on to E.

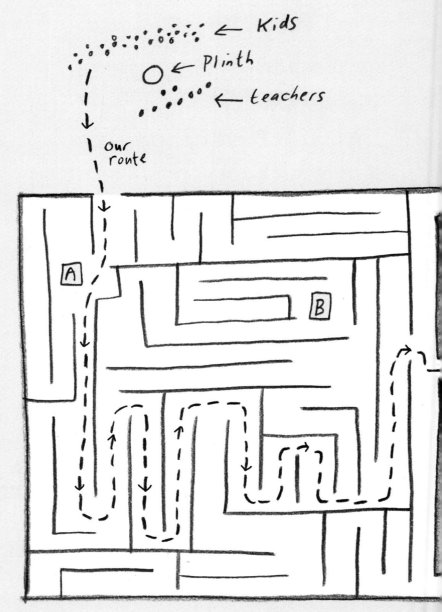

Kids ←

Plinth ←

teachers ←

our route

A

B

At E, the trail ended in a
small pile of sand.

Then — **nothing**.

*Where had they gone?*

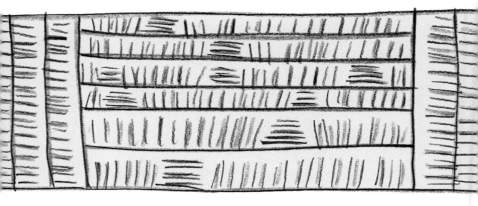

We looked up at the
shelves for more clues.

All the books began with
the letter *E*.

*No surprise there.*

**And then we saw it!**

A massive volume titled
*Egyptology — A Most
Boring Book.*

There was something *weird* about that book.

I mean, how could Egyptology be ***boring***? It didn't add up.

I reached for it.

As I pulled it out,
something amazing
happened.

A **trapdoor** opened up
between me and Rob.

And then with a slight
mechanical whirr,
**up came a ladder!**

We looked down the hole,
then at each other,
and in we went.

*Best friends sometimes
don't need words to
communicate.*

Down and down
and down and
down and down
and down and
down and down
and down and
down and down
and down and
down and down
and down and
down and down
and down and
down and down
and down and
down and down
and down and
down and down
and down and
down and down
and down and down
and down and down
and down and down
and down and down
and down and down
and down and
down and down and
down and down and
down and down and
and down and down and
down and down and down.

We emerged into some kind of *storage room.*

A secret basement!

And there was Mr. Sniffy's *boreholicopter*!

SNIFFSONIAN

Suddenly my KB-15 started
flashing **like crazy**.

And then we saw them!

*Mr. Sniffy* and
*Devil-Cat* with the
**Amazing Ideas Box!**

They looked up.

"Dash Candoo?" asked
Mr. Sniffy with a sneer.

*"Dash Can-**Don't**!"*
replied Devil-Cat
with an **evil grin**.

As they spoke,
**Desert-Scallywags**
emerged from the
basement shadows.

Again they went into
**Move #26,941 (Sandstorm).**

But this time they were
*fast* and there were no
compost bins to save us.

# We were caught!

"The ideas are now MINE!
Mwahahahahahha!"
Sniffy laughed.

From within our
swirling, sandy prison
we watched **helplessly**
as Sniffy, Devil-Cat, and
the scallywags squashed
into the boreholicopter
and entered their escape
tunnel.

# Trapped

*inside* a sandstorm,
*in* a hidden basement,
*below* a library maze.

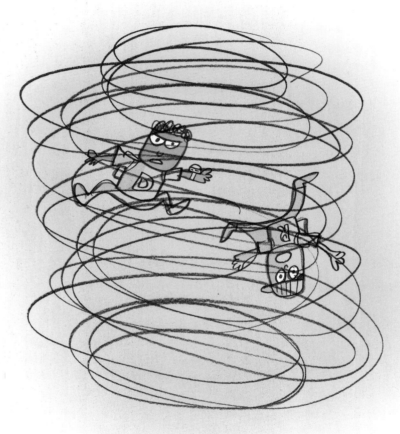

*This was not good.*
***VERY not good.***

# Chapter 9

# The Chase

Meanwhile, up in the library, Greta had *calmed* Ms. Grimstead *down* by *jamming* Mr. Darling's pet **pinkfish** onto her head.

This reduced the lump swelling, and the fish were *fascinated*.

There wasn't much Mr. Darling could do because he's **totally terrified** of Grimstead.

As things settled
down ever so slightly,
Greta realized Rob and I
had ***totally*** disappeared.

She had to find us!

Suddenly she remembered
Sniffy's tunnel from
earlier in the day.

She figured it had to have
something to do with
this mayhem!

# Then she had an idea!

She *sprinted* back to the
hole-digging field, *jumped*
into our Aardvark 66,
and *headed* straight down.

As Greta searched for Sniffy's tunnel, the macro-map began to show the outline of something new:

a hidden room *deep below* the library!

# The secret basement!

And in she burst.

Working *calmly* and *quickly*,
Greta clicked the switch
on the Aardvark's
<u>*Full-Vacuum Snozzle*</u> *(FVS)*.

She turned the dial to
**FULL DEPLOYMENT**, and
*whoosh*, the sandstorm was
sucked up.

Rob and I
jumped in
and *quickly*
filled Greta
in on what
had just
happened.

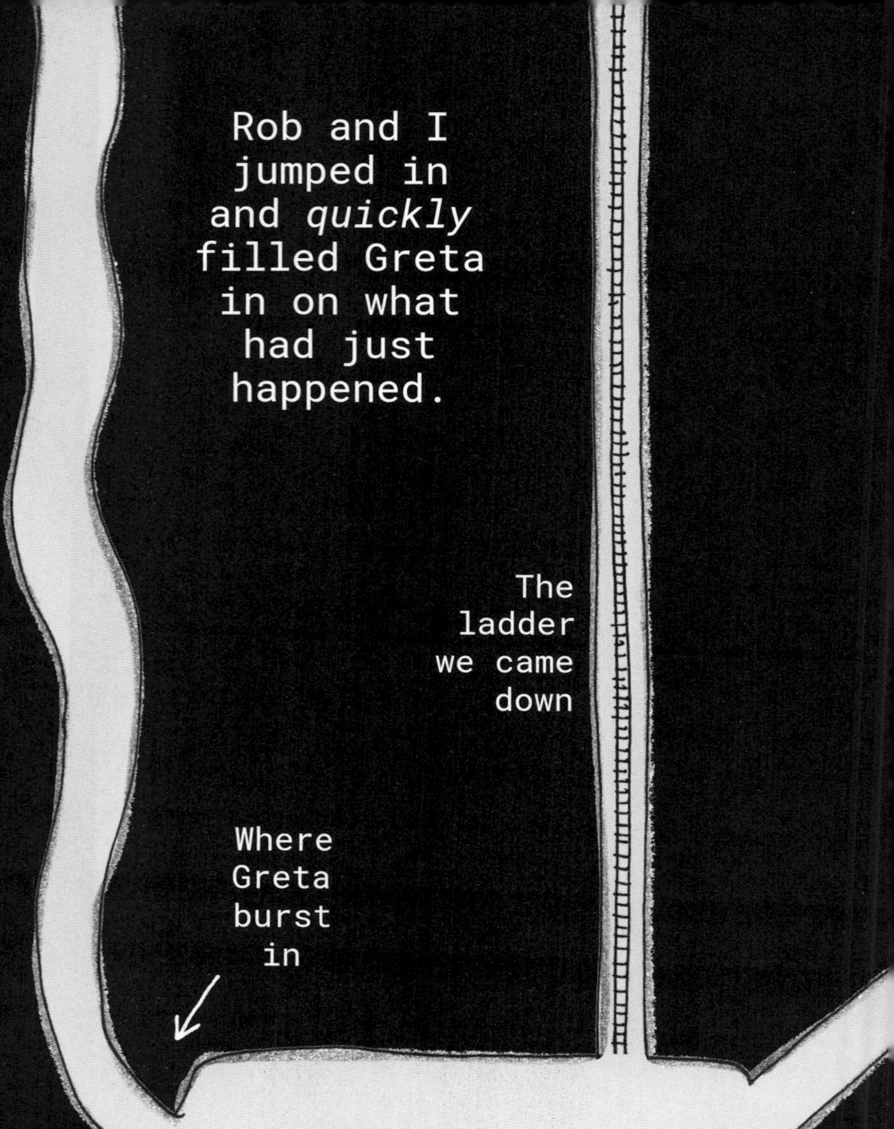

The
ladder
we came
down

Where
Greta
burst
in

Then we set off
in *hot pursuit* of the
thieves, as *fast* as we
could go!

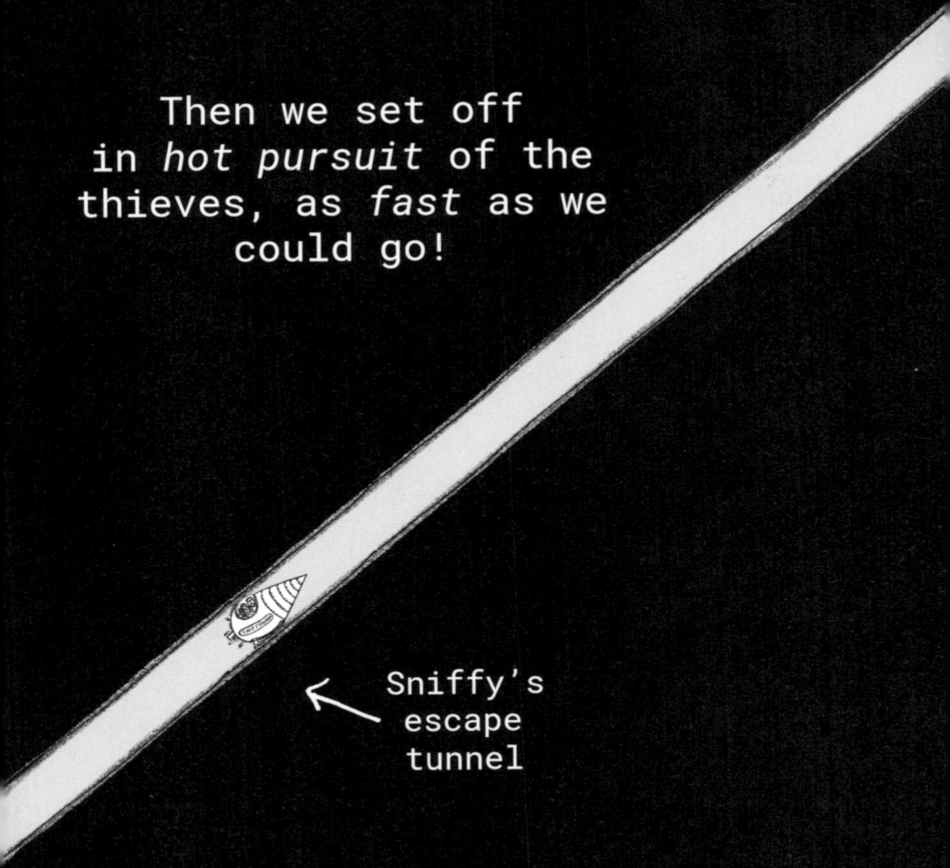

← Sniffy's
escape
tunnel

Luckily the Aardvark 66 is
a MUCH faster digger than a
boreholicopter, and Greta is
an **AMAZING** digger-driver.

Making a separate side
tunnel, we overtook Sniffy,

and then entered his tunnel
**ahead of him.**

Greta slowly started
steering our own route,
**upward and back to school.**

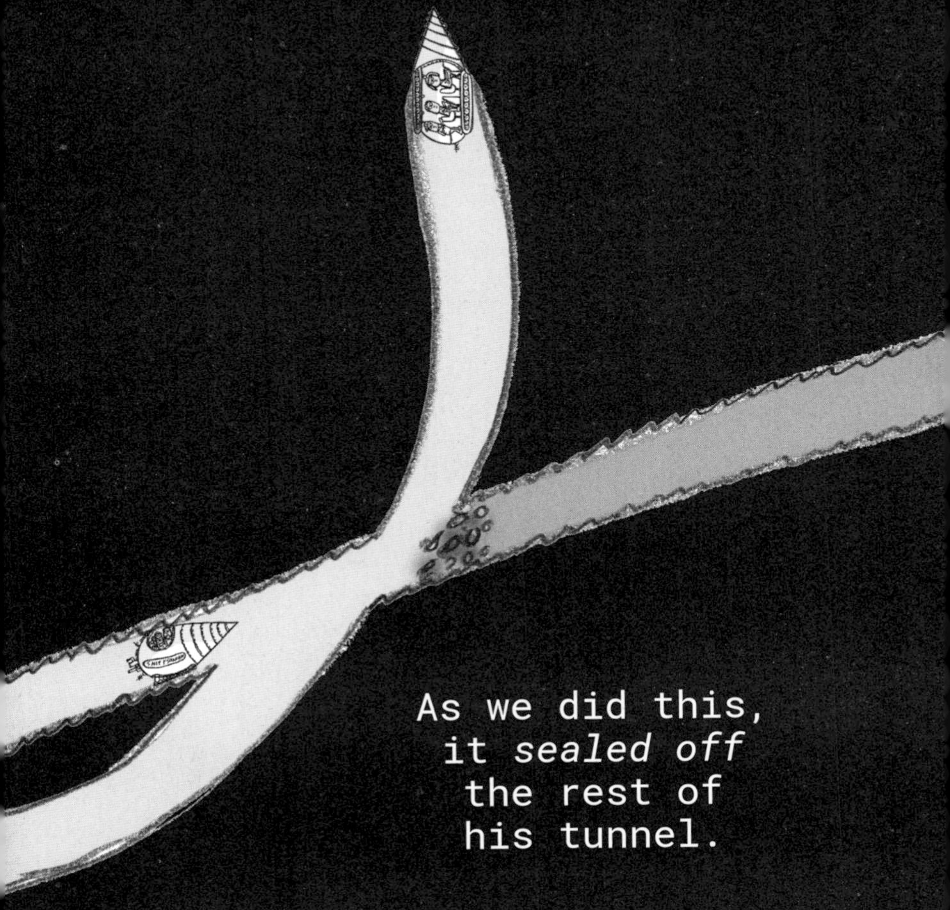

As we did this,
it *sealed off*
the rest of
his tunnel.

# It worked!

He was following
us back to
the library
*without even
realizing it.*

We emerged to a **CFATMS**
*(Continued Full And
Total Mayhem Situation)*
in the library.

A VERY SURPRISED
Mr. Sniffy emerged
*straight behind us!*

Now it was HIS turn to be *frozen in shock.*

(But not Devil-Cat, who'd disappeared back down the tunnel with the stinky scallywags. *We'll get you next time, Devil-Cat!*)

Pointing accusingly at
Mr. Sniffy, Greta yelled,
**"He has the Amazing
Ideas Box!"**

Everyone gasped.

Sniffy, caught *red-handed*,
had no choice but to
climb out of the
hole-digger **and confess.**

# Chapter 10

# The Winner

Ant #4,658,
in case you
were wondering

The Official Confession of
## Mr. P. R. Sniffy,
Sniffsonian Owner & Curator
(PhD, U. of West-Hosnollia)

"When the Aqualinia Water Park opened
next door, the number of visitors coming to
the Sniffsonian Museum went right down
to nought, zero, zilch.

I was desperate for a way to get vistors
back to the museum. So I arranged to visit
Swedhump Elementary on the same day as
Ms. Aqualine, to find a way to steal the
waterslide ideas.

My plan was to use the ideas to make
my own waterslide, not outside,
but INSIDE the museum.

I confess, I'd do ANYTHING
to keep kids visiting the Sniffsonian."

When he finished, he started
to cry. **A lot.**

Large blobs of *tears and
snot* were hitting the
carpet, and Ms. Grimstead's
**lump** *began to swell again*.

Gronville
Honkersmith
started
crying too
for some
reason.

Then, surprisingly, *and luckily*, Ms. Aqualine did something **astounding**.

She shushed everyone, including Mr. Sniffy.

Slowly and quietly, she said she actually

# LOVED

Mr. Sniffy's idea.

"Imagine a waterslide
*IN* a museum?!!!"
she said.

And actually, we couldn't
help but agree that it
was a **VERY** good idea.

"Mr. Sniffy,"
said Ms. Aqualine,
**"I forgive you!"**

Sniffy smiled.

Everyone **cheered**.
*Even* the lump.
*Even* the pinkfish
(but not Gronville).

Ms. Aqualine then gently took the Amazing Ideas Box from Mr. Sniffy and placed it back on the plinth.

## "Time to announce the winner!"
she declared.

We held our breaths.

"ALL entries win!"

"Pardon me?"

"ALL entries win!"
she repeated happily.

"There was only space for **ONE**
new slide in MY park, **but we
can have LOTS in the HUGE
Sniffsonian!"**

Some
of the **amazing**
winning entries were:

Shereena's **Rainforest Waterslide**!

My **Cloud Waterslide**!

And pride of place...

Greta's **Cleopatra's Waterslide**!

"We're going to build them ALL!"
Ms. Aqualine shouted.

Everyone cheered again.

Even Mr. Sniffy.

*And even Gronville this time!*

And that's why, if you ever go to the Sniffsonian, you'll see a LOT of waterslides there. **That's what makes it not only the world's most FAMOUS museum, but the most POPULAR too!**

A few years later, Ms. Aqualine and Mr. Sniffy actually **got married**, but that's a story for another time.

Then the bell rang,
and school was over.

# Time to go home!

## The end.

### 3D Macro-map

Aardvark hole-diggers come equipped with 3-dimensional macro-maps. These allow the user to see exactly where they are when underground. Radar functionality allows them to see through the ground to other machines and other tunnels, with a range of 25 miles. Infra-red functionality allows them to assess soil type and density at a range of up to 5 miles. Infra-green functionality allows them to spot living/breathing creatures underground with a range of up to 1 mile.

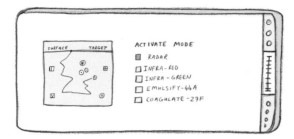

### Aardvark 4.2D

Dash and Rob won one of these in a secret competition (so unfortunately we are unable to give any information about how they actually won it). It has a 4.2-liter diesel engine with a built-in turbo-electric wassoon-emulsifier, so it's good for stealth and speed, but not great on endurance. They keep it parked in Swedhump Elementary's orange grove.

Engine size: 4.2-liter (diesel)
Number of blades: 1
Max speed: 50 mph
Max distance on one tank: 25 miles
Strength/Special feature: Superfast
Electric version available soon.

### Aardvark 66

Spacious two-person hole-digger that comes equipped with a 3D Macro-map and a Full-Vacuum Snozzle.

Engine size: 6.6-liter (diesel)
Number of blades: 1
Max speed: 20 mph
Max distance on one tank: 100 miles
Strength/Special feature: Fantastic endurance
Electric version available soon.

### Advanced Pause Strategy (APS)

To acquire Pause Master certification, the candidate needs to perfect APS. This involves four main steps:

[1] Learning the entire Pauselopedia by heart
[2] Spending six months in a cave on top of a mountain with a Pause Guru
[3] Perfecting the Gold-Star Tips of that particular Pause Guru
[4] Getting through the preliminary knockout round of the Pause Game World Championships

### Almanac

The COMPLETE ALMANAC is the place where you can find out everything about Dash and his world. It's online here: total-mayhem.com/almanac
What you're reading now is the Book 4 Almanac, providing detailed information for this book only.

### Andri Grimminik

Andri Grimminik Herr-Groggen-Chommen-Hummen-Grekken is arguably the world's most famous water fountain designer. He was born in Slovoslochuckia and makes fountains for the rich and famous worldwide. His cousin's son's friend's sister's uncle's aunt's friend's neighbor's dad's brother's friend's daughter's daughter's daughter's daughter's daughter attended Swedhump Elementary.

Famous clients of his include: King Edmond the Gurkk, Queen Jezebel of South-Northern Swottolia, The Bog-Slotnigg Water Park, President William Williamson of Williamsville.

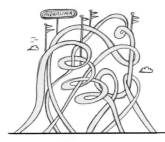

### Aqualinia Water Park

Probably the world's best waterslide park. Ms. Aqualine is the founding chairwoman of the Aqualine Corporation, which established the water park in 2019. The Aqualine Corporation is also renowned for its pool floaties, which are sold worldwide. The pinkfish, sweds, and osteops are particularly popular.

### Armadillo Cake

Totally, totally, totally, totally, totally, totally, totally, totally, totally, totally, delicious armadillo-flavored cake. Shaped like an armadillo.

Armadillo cakes come in eight sizes:
[1] Very large
[2] Large
[3] Large medium
[4] Medium medium
[5] Small medium
[6] Small
[7] Tiny
[8] Microscopic
The last two sizes are not really worth getting, except for
your ants.

### Boreholicopter

Extraordinary machine that can fly and dig
holes. Very expensive and very few have
been built. Equipped with a subterranean
ossifier, quadro-retractable rotors, and
a multifunctional-dual-reticulated glocken-
sprocket.

### Butterfly-cam-drone

Small, easily deployed pocket camera drone that is
shaped like a butterfly.
Infra-red, green, blue, and purple technology enabled.
Return-to-base functionality.
Range of up to 25 miles.
Can be operated by remote control, or mind control if pilot
has an XS-42 microchip embedded in their head.

### Clod Tickler 64

1-person hole-digger.
Engine size: 6.4-liter (regular gas)
Number of blades: 2
Max speed: 30 mph
Max distance on one tank: 20 miles
Strength/Special feature: Decent speed but superb digging
ability. Can also be used to cut down fences and trees.

### Desert-Scallywags

How common: Moderate
Special power: Create sandstorms, desert survival
Weaknesses: Tend to scatter sand wherever they go.
Do not like to be laughed at. Quite scared of spiders.
Typical group size: 7 or more
Operate alone? Never
Maximum jump distance: 6 feet
Cleverness: 7/10
Speed: 3/10
Agility: 5/10

### Devil-Cat
*Huge double-tailed black cat that always*
*lands on the wrong side of the law.*
*Tends to partner with criminals.*
*Fears nothing but fruit.*
*Terrified of watermelons.*
*However, he loves vegetables,*
*especially carrots.*

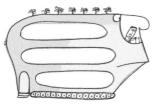

### FiCTaP Mode
Acronym for **F**ind **C**lues, **T**rack, **a**nd **P**ursue.
This is not classified as an actual combat move.
Regarded as a key asset, which is why it is taught as a
year one course at most academies for stealth operatives.
The sub-modes of FiCTaP Mode are as follows:
[1] FiC: Look for clues anywhere. Be creative and think
    differently. Don't accept normal as normal. Fugitives
    aim to trick you.
[2] T: Track. Follow the clues, but be prepared for them to
    disappear or change. Good tracking involves patience and
    attention to detail. Having a snack with you also helps.
[3] P: Pursuit. Three types:
    [a] Stealth Pursuit – Your target does not know he/she/they/it
        is being followed.
    [b] Active Live Pursuit – Your target has spotted you.
    [c] Confidential – Sorry but we can't give any details on
        this, as you don't have security-clearance 56/foxtrot.

### Flus
*Flying bus – powered by 5 to 10 RRRs*
*(Retractable Rooftop Rotors)*
*Top air speed: 333 mph*
*Top ground speed: 55 mph*
*Maximum capacity: 44, excluding pilot*
*Max altitude: 3,333 feet*
*Typical color: Yellow with yellow spots*

### Full-Vacuum Snozzle (FVS)
*Large vacuum hose with turbo-charged suction ossicle attached. Can*

*be purchased as a stand-alone unit (like a*
*lawnmower or household vacuum cleaner)*
*or as a vehiculated extra feature*
*(e.g., the Aardvark 66 hole-*
*digger has one).*
*Suction capacity standard model:*
*366 viento-watts*
*Suction capacity premium model:*
*588 viento-watts*

### Heemo-globule globules

These are small, very rare, highly precious globules
containing heemo-globules, which are mined all over
the world.

### Hole-diggers

The two most common versions are the Aardvark 4.2D (used by Dash
and Rob) and the Aardvark 5.2rg (preferred by criminals).

### Invizizz

An invizizz is a type of stinging insect. They
are completely silent, and their venom causes localized
invisibility. They only sting when they are grumpy, but —
unfortunately they are grumpy 77 percent of the time.
The other 23 percent of the time they are asleep.

### KB-15

Imminent Danger Warning Device (IDWD)
KB-15 Flash Codes:
* Red — on-off 1-second intervals continuous:
Imminent danger
* Red — on 2s, off 2s: Imminent lightning storm
* Green — on 3s, off 1s: Takeout delivery almost here
* Blue — on 5s, off 5s: Battery needs charging

### Move #84 (Tarantula)

This is a highly effective evasive maneuver, particularly
useful against Desert-Scallywags, as they are scared of
spiders. The move involves a deep grimace and spiderlike
screaming combined with a rapid and continuous flailing. The
louder the scream and faster the flail, the more effective
this move is.

### Move #6,745 (Rocket-launch)

This is a highly dangerous 1-4-1-1 attack move. Often used
by Desert-Scallywags. It involves building a tower with the
strongest "foundation" scallywag at the bottom. Four fighters
then balance off him or her, to form the "base" of the rocket,
then the two most agile of them stand atop each other to form

the "nose cone." The launch involves the top
two flying off at high speed into the attack. The
base four then attack and the foundation scallywag
remains in place.

### Move #26,941 (Sandstorm)

This is a very, very dangerous
move that involves conjuring
up a sandstorm. It is the favorite attack
move of Desert-Scallywags since they always
have a trail of sand following them. Once in
formation, the scallywags raise their arms and
begin a rapid repeat chant that sounds like a
mixture between a humming snail and a toad with
stomach cramps. As they do this, they stretch
out and sway their arms, which lifts and twirls
any sand in the area. It forms a mini tornado
that catches anything in its path. The conjured
sandstorm is impregnable and remains in place
for at least 24 hours. The only known remedy is
for it to be sucked up by a vacuum snozzle.
Some hole-diggers come with built-in snozzles
specifically for this purpose.

### Pause Game

Highly social, brilliant, and occasionally annoying game. First
recorded occurrence of it was in ancient Hipposwotania in 467 BC.
The game has been refined over generations and the rules are now
codified in the Pauselopedia. The basic rules are as follows:

**RULE 1:** When someone shouts, "Pause!" everyone in the room has
to freeze completely still, including the person
who shouted "Pause!"

**RULE 2:** You can only move again when the
shouter shouts, "Play!"

**RULE 3:** The shouter needs to hold their breath
between shouting "Pause!" and "Play!"

**RULE 4:** If the shouter breathes before they
say "Play!" the "Pause!" is broken
and everyone can move again.

**RULE 5:** Each person is only allowed to shout "Pause!"
once per day, and they can do it whenever they want.

### Pause Game World Championships

Held annually.
Prizes as follows:
1st place: Gold medal + $5,000,006
2nd place: Silver medal + $2,000,006
3rd place: Bronze medal + $1,000,003
4th place: Copper medal + $100 + 5 gallons of wombat juice
5th place: No prize
6th place: Aluminum medal + a bag of carrots (nice ones)

## Pauselopedia

*Written by Zephaniah Rrr-Tökk-Tökk, this fine tome covers everything there is to know about the Pause Game. Large sections on rules, history, national, variants, famous competitions, legendary winners, and notorious cheats.*

*The first edition was published in 1995. New editions are published annually. There were only 100 copies of the first edition, which these days are highly sought after and VERY expensive. At a recent auction in Johannesburg, one sold for $33 million.*

## Perforator 800

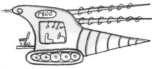

*One- or two-person hole-digger.*
*Engine size: 8-liter (diesel)*
*Number of blades: 3*
*Max speed: 5 mph*
*Max distance on one tank: 10 miles*
*Strength/Special feature: Slow-moving, terrifying beast. Can dig through most surfaces, including asphalt.*

## P'tonk-45

*Mechanized library chair. Only two known to exist. One is owned by Ms. Grimstead.*
*The other was formerly owned by King Edmond the Gurkk, but it got stolen. Its whereabouts are completely unknown. Sadly.*

## Pinkfish

*Like goldfish, but a different color. Pink, actually. Very tame when happy, but when bored can be aggressive and bite like piranhas.*
*Need constant attention, i.e., have to be walked, entertained, read to before bed, etc. Some rich pinkfish actually have their own walk-bowls. (Walk-bowls are bowls that can walk, in case you were wondering.)*

## Sniffsonian Museum
World's most famous and important museum of natural history,
artifacts, trivia, miscellany, and heemo-globule globules.
It is also famous for its epic cafeteria.

## Snolly juice
Snolly juice is the perfect accompaniment to snorridge.
Its name is actually an acronym for the ingredients.

**SNO**: Snow
**L**: Lemon juice
**L**: Linguini
**Y**: Yogurt

## Snorridge
Snorridge is like porridge, but better. It's like normal
porridge, but made with snow. If you don't live in a snowy
place, you can buy your own snorridge snow maker and have it
in the kitchen. If you do live in a snowy place, better to
use fresh snow.

Often accompanied by a glass of fresh snolly juice.

Most supermarkets stock snorridge, but demand would be so
high if it was on a normal shelf that it's usually tucked
away on a secret shelf. If you go to the cereal section in a
regular supermarket and stand right in the middle of the
display and you then pull away the boxes at belly button
level, usually that's where the secret shelf is located.

### Staircase Moose

*Friendly creatures that can be tamed and become very useful for assistance with reaching things. Same life span as humans. The staircase is not there when born, and usually only starts growing once the moose reaches the teenage years. Large herds of them are found in the northern reaches of Moremi Forest.*

### Stumpnose Elementary

*Principal: Professor-Inspector Josiah Stumpnose*
*Rival school to Swedhump Elementary.*
*Smells of sardines in some areas.*
*Most kids who attend this school are known to be:*
*[1] awful or*
*[2] rude or*
*[3] mean or*
*[4] have terrible table manners or*
*[5] all of the above.*

### Swedhump Elementary

*Dash's school.*
*Principal: Mrs. Rosebank*
*Probably the best school in the world.*
*Definitely has the best teachers in the world.*
*Named after the hump of a swed, a two-faced humped creature.*

### Tie-D-Yupper

*Highly useful and effective device that tidies everything up. Range is 12 meters. Can only be used once per 24 hours. If used twice, the second time it actually doubles the mess.*

### Trenchifyer 98

*One- or two-person hole-digger.*
*Engine size: 9.8-liter (regular gas)*
*Number of blades: 2*
*Max speed: 10 mph*
*Max distance on one tank: 17 miles*
*Strength/Special feature:*
*Perfect for surface work, like digging trenches or swimming holes*

### Triplocopter

Triple-helicopters invented by G. & J.
Tarrow Siblings Inc. in 2010. The equivalent
of three helicopters stuck together. They
are sixty-one times faster and seventeen times
more powerful than regular helicopters, though
more complicated to fly. The test pilot of the first
version was James Hogsbottom, who teaches Paper Airplane
Class at Swedhump Elementary. There have been no reported
triplocopter crashes to date.

### Twoaster

A twoaster is a toaster that takes 12 slices of bread.
The numbers on the eject dial refer to height in meters.
So if you set it to 12, once done,
the toast will fly at least 12
meters high. Can be useful in
combat situations.

### Vibrating Cockroach of
### Awfulness (VCA)

VCAs can be found in any terrain and under almost any cir-
cumstances. And regrettably, they can fly. Their vibrations
initially are harmless, but if allowed to continue for over
6 minutes (i.e., 360 seconds), everything just starts to feel
awful. Scientists are so far not able to explain it.

Examples of the awfulness:
[1] If you are baking a cake and a VCA is undetected in the
    area, the cake will taste awful.
[2] If you go to the hairdresser and a VCA is in the
    vicinity, your hair will look awful.
[3] If you're singing in a concert and a VCA is somewhere in
    the room, you will sound awful.

# FOR DASH CANDOO, EVERY DAY IS . . .
# TOTAL MAYHEM!

## ABOUT THE CREATORS

*Ralph Lazar & Lisa Swerling live in California.*

*Ralph made up the Dash stories (inspired by wrestling his godson — Dash!) and did the drawings. Lisa shaped the stories into this book.*

*Ralph & Lisa are* New York Times *bestselling authors, and the creators of the popular illustrated project* Happiness Is..., *which has been translated into over twenty languages and has over three million followers online.*

Their studio website is lastlemon.com

Ralph is also a painter, and Lisa makes miniature worlds in boxes.

Ralph's art website: ralphlazar.com

Lisa's art website: glasscathedrals.com

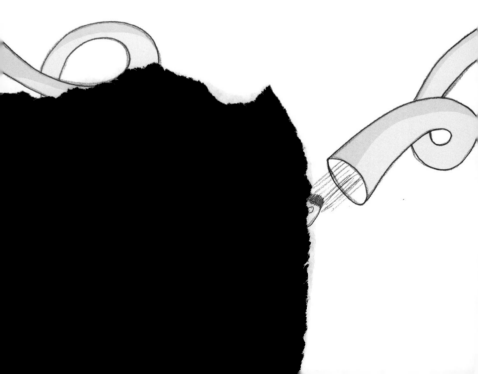